Alien
Adver

Trapped in Time

Elen Caldecott • Jonatronix

OXFORD
UNIVERSITY PRESS

Max's mission log

We are travelling through space on board the micro-ship Excelsa with our new friend, Eight.

We are trying to get home. Our only chance is to get to the Waythroo Wormhole – a space tunnel that should lead us back to our own galaxy. We don't have long. The wormhole is due to collapse very soon. If we don't get there in time, we'll be trapped in the Delta-Zimmer Galaxy forever!

To make matters worse, a space villain called Badlaw is following us in his Destroyer ship. Badlaw and his army of robotic Krools want to take over Earth. We can't let that happen!

Our new mission is simple: to shake off Badlaw and get to the Waythroo Wormhole before it collapses. I just wish it was as easy as it sounds.

Time until wormhole collapses: 4 days, 11 hours and 2 minutes

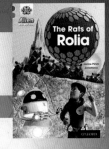

In our last adventure ...

The Excelsa was running low on lintum
– a crystal used to power its computers.
We landed on Planet Grenin, hoping to
find some more. Ant, Eight and I went
off in search of lintum. Cat and Tiger
stayed on board the Excelsa.

The Excelsa was carried away by an
army of red rats. They wanted the
ship's computer. Cat and Tiger had to
teleport to safety. Meanwhile, Ant, Eight
and I met some friendly green rats.

Then our old friend Reeba arrived in his
space pod! He offered to give the red
rats the energy core from his ship if they
agreed to leave the planet. The green
rats gave us a present – a box of
lintum! Now we have enough to
power the computers for the rest of
our journey.

Chapter 1 – A strange light

Cat gazed at the sparkling stars all around her. It was her first spacewalk.

"Come on, Cat," Tiger said. "We've got a job to do."

The ship had been attacked by rats back on Planet Grenin, and Cat and Tiger were checking for any serious damage.

Cat turned to face Tiger. "Sorry," she said. "It's just so amazing out here."

Cat glanced past Tiger, towards the front of the ship.

"Tiger," she whispered, "what's that?"

A flash of yellow light had appeared just in front of the Excelsa, crackling and sparking with energy. Then, just as quickly, the light disappeared. It left behind a rippling area of darkness, as if a stone had been dropped into a puddle of black water.

Immediately, the ship started to slow down. Then it stopped. It was surrounded by an area of blackness that seemed to pulse like a heartbeat.

"Cat calling bridge!" she yelled into the mouthpiece in her helmet. "Can anyone hear me?"

There was no reply.

"Let's get back inside," Tiger said. "We need to find out what's happening."

The two friends made their way as fast as they could across the surface of the ship, back to the exit hatch. As they walked, the blackness around the ship continued to pulse.

Back inside, Cat and Tiger removed their helmets and hurried towards the bridge.

Halfway along the corridor, they saw Ant. He was talking to Max on the communi-screen.

"Ant, did you see that light?" Tiger said, hurrying over to him. "Can we run some tests to find out what it was?"

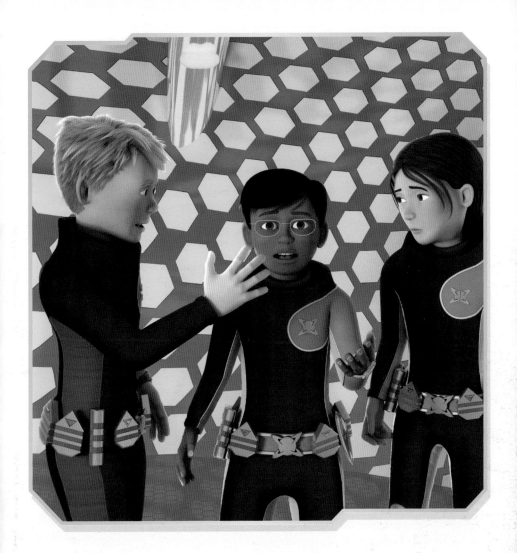

Ant spoke into the screen. "No sign of them yet," he said.

"OK. Keep a look-out," came the reply from Max.

"Ant?" Cat said. "We're right here!"

Ant didn't reply. Tiger waved his hand in front of Ant's face, but Ant didn't even blink.

Cat and Tiger tried to get Ant's attention but he just stared blankly at the screen.

After a few minutes, Ant spoke into the communi-screen again. "No sign of them yet," he said.

"OK. Keep a look-out," Max replied.

Cat looked at Ant. "You just said that!"

"It's like they're on a loop," said Tiger.

"Let's get to the bridge and find out what's going on," Cat said.

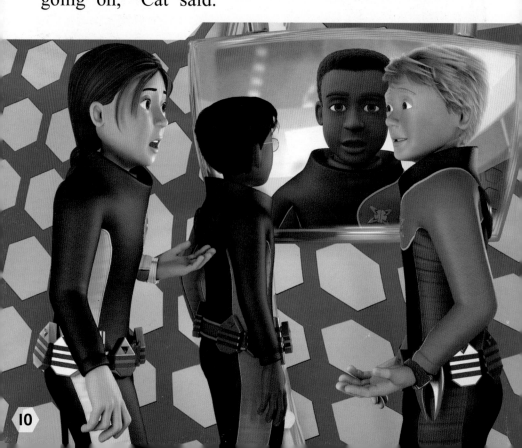

At first glance, everything on the bridge appeared to be normal. Eight was in the pilot's seat, steering the ship, and Max was at his desk.

"Max, are you OK?" Tiger asked. "Can you hear me?"

Max didn't respond.

Just then, Ant's voice came through Max's communi-screen. "No sign of them yet."

"OK. Keep a look-out," Max replied.

"Eight, something weird is happening," Tiger said. "Max and Ant are stuck in a loop."

Eight didn't react. Instead, she turned to Max. "Has Ant reported back yet?" she said.

"Whatever is happening has affected Eight, too," Cat said to Tiger. "She can't see or hear us."

"*WARNING! Time rift*," the ship suddenly announced.

"What's a time rift?" asked Cat.

"Let's try and find out," Tiger said. He hurried to his desk and started tapping buttons.

In seconds, information filled the viewscreen.

Time rifts

Time rifts are small rips in the fabric of the universe, which can stop or bend time. They occur when two galactical vectors (invisible lines of energy that criss-cross the galaxy) intersect. At this point the fabric of space becomes weak.

Effect
A ship that is stuck in a time rift will repeat the same point in time until it is released.

Solution
A blast of around one billion mega-whumps fired into the rift will release a trapped ship.

Formation

Time rifts are very rare. They can be small and difficult to detect. Once the rips have been formed they can grow, pulsing with 'dark light'.

"The ship is stuck in a time rift!" Tiger said. "That's why everyone's repeating what they're saying."

"Why aren't we affected?" Cat asked.

Tiger shrugged. "We were outside at the back of the ship when we flew into the rift. Maybe that had something to do with it."

"The computer says that we need a massive energy blast to set us free. How are we going to create a blast big enough?" Cat asked fearfully.

"I don't know. The Excelsa doesn't have enough power to get out by itself," Tiger replied.

Just then, Cat noticed his watch was flashing a red warning. "Tiger, your watch!" she cried.

Tiger checked the monitor. "It's the Destroyer!" he said. "Badlaw's nearby, and this time we can't get away!"

Chapter 3 – Finding the energy

Cat ran to her desk. An image of the Destroyer filled her screen. "Badlaw's catching up," she reported, "but he's not reached the rift yet."

"It's only a matter of time before he finds us," said Tiger.

Just then, they heard Ant's voice from the communi-screen. "No sign of them yet," he said.

"OK. Keep a look-out," Max replied.

"I wish they'd stop saying that every five minutes," Cat said.

"Five minutes …" Tiger said thoughtfully. "That's it, Cat! I've got an idea. How long will it take for Badlaw to get here?"

"Not long, he's pretty close," replied Cat, a little confused.

"In that case, follow me!" Tiger called as he raced for the door. Cat chased after him.

Tiger ran to the teleport room and headed for the controls.

"What's your idea?" Cat asked, panting to catch her breath.

"The rift is making the Excelsa reset every five minutes," Tiger said. "That means we have exactly four minutes and fifty-nine seconds."

"Four minutes and fifty-nine seconds to do what?" Cat asked.

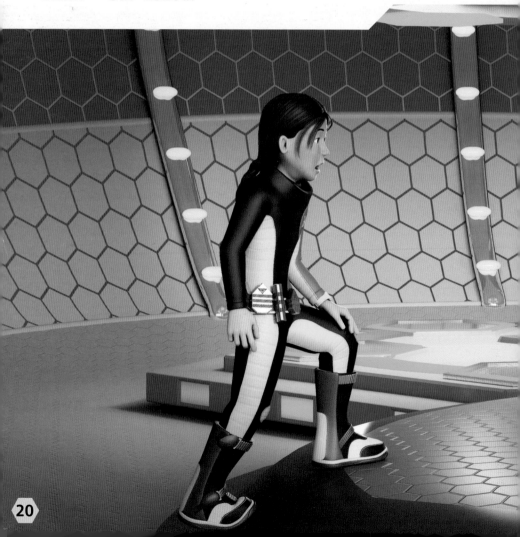

"To find one billion mega-whumps of energy," Tiger answered with a grin.

"I'm going to activate the teleport as soon as the next loop starts. Then we'll have the maximum amount of time to complete our mission before it resets."

"Where are you sending us?" Cat asked.

"The Destroyer."

"What?" said Cat, with a shudder. "You seriously want us to go on board that ship again?"

The last time they had been on Badlaw's Destroyer they had only narrowly escaped.

Tiger nodded. "That's my plan. I'm sure Badlaw's ship has got enough power to get us out of this time rift," he explained. "We just need to wait for the Destroyer to come within teleport range."

Chapter 4 – Follow the Krools

There was a deep rumbling as the Destroyer came nearer. The micro-ship began to shudder.

Tiger looked at Cat. "Ready?" he asked.

Cat took a deep breath. "As ready as I'll ever be."

"I've linked the teleport to my watch, so I can get us back," Tiger explained. "As long as it's before the five minutes are up."

He engaged the teleport and the friends felt themselves begin to fade.

The next moment, Cat and Tiger found themselves aboard the Destroyer. They were in some kind of cargo hold, with crates towering around them. They hit their watches and grew to normal size.

Cat checked her watch. "Four minutes and forty-eight seconds remaining," she said.

Suddenly an alarm wailed. When it stopped, the friends heard the sound of metal scraping against metal.

"Krools!" Tiger warned.

Cat and Tiger ducked out of sight behind a stack of crates.

A huge screen flickered. Badlaw's mean
face appeared.

"Attention all Krools!" he screeched. "Prepare
to capture the Excelsa! Move to battle stations
and charge the energy wrench."

The energy wrench was Badlaw's tractor
beam. He used it to pull spaceships towards the
Destroyer so he could take control of them.

"We have to stop them before Badlaw pulls the Excelsa into his claws!" Cat whispered.

"Do we?" Tiger said with a grin.

"What do you mean?" she asked.

"If we could find a way to reverse the energy wrench, then instead of pulling the Excelsa in, it would push the ship out of the time rift," Tiger explained.

"It's a good idea ... Let's get to work," whispered Cat bravely.

Cautiously, Tiger peered out from behind a crate. He saw a patrol of Krools rolling past like giant marbles, all headed in one direction. "They look like they know where they're going, and I bet it's to the energy wrench," he said. "We need to follow those Krools!"

Tiger stood up, but Cat grabbed his arm.

"Wait," she said. "A micro-mission will be much safer!"

Cat hit the button on her watch and shrank. Tiger quickly followed.

They both engaged their holo-wings and followed the Krools at a safe distance.

Chapter 5 – In control

Cat and Tiger soon found themselves in a large room filled with lots of machines. One machine was much larger than the rest. It looked like some kind of rocket and was directed at a large circular hole in the wall.

Just then, Badlaw's face appeared on a screen again. "Krools, prepare the energy wrench!"

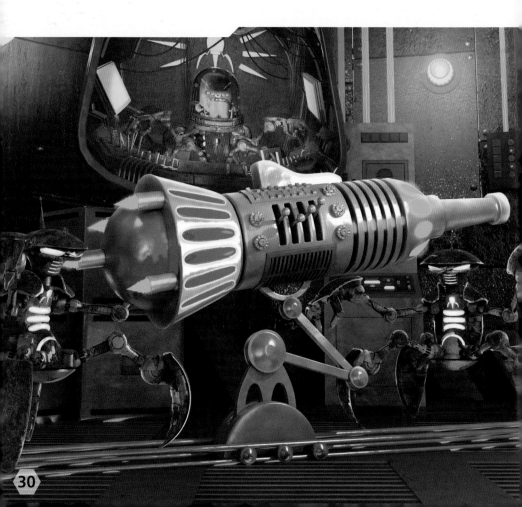

The Krools quickly gathered around the energy
wrench, hurriedly flicking switches and levers and
turning various dials. One by one, a series of
energy bars lit up as the energy wrench began
to charge.

Unnoticed by the busy Krools, Cat and Tiger
flew close to the wrench.

Tiger looked at the energy bars. "It looks
like it's got the energy we need ... one
billion mega-whumps!"

"Are you sure it won't damage the Excelsa?" Cat asked.

"Not if we programme the reversal just right," Tiger replied.

"We need to get to the controls then," Cat checked her watch, "and we only have three minutes left."

"Follow me!" Tiger cried. He twisted in the air and dived down towards the energy wrench.

"In here," he said. He aimed for a vent in the side of the machine and flew through a narrow gap.

The inside of the machine was covered in circuit boards. Tiger studied one of the boards in silence. A tangle of wires led from the floor up to a series of red ports at the top of the board.

"Do you know what to do?" Cat asked.

"Yes, I think so," Tiger replied.

"You think?" Cat said. "You need to be certain, Tiger. Otherwise it's too risky."

Below each of the red ports was an empty blue port.

"We need to rewire each of these connections," explained Tiger. With trembling fingers, he traced a single red wire across the circuit board. When he reached the other end of it, he gripped the rubber tubing and tugged hard.

"Plug this red end into that blue port," Tiger said to Cat. He handed her the end of the wire.

She flew down and shoved the loose wire into an empty port.

Then Tiger pulled out another red wire and put it into a second empty, blue port.

Chapter 6 – Time's up

"There's only one more to go," Tiger said. He pulled and tugged at the last wire. It wouldn't budge.

"Come on, Tiger!" Cat cried.

"Just a minute!" he replied.

"We haven't got a minute!" wailed Cat.

Suddenly, the energy wrench whirred as it began to slowly twist and turn. Then it moved towards the hole in the wall, making a screeching noise as it slid along the rails on the floor.

"Begin countdown!" Badlaw's voice responded. "Ten, nine, eight ..."

Inside the control panel, Cat grabbed hold of the wire too. It was completely stuck.

"Heave!" Tiger yelled.

They strained as hard as they could, but the wire remained firmly in place.

"It's no use," Cat said. "Even our combined strength won't shift it."

"Engage power boots!" Tiger yelled.

They pressed the buttons on their suits and blue energy shot out from below their feet. They gave one last tug, using all their effort.

Suddenly, the wire popped free. Cat held the loose end in her hands.

"Five, four, three …" Badlaw gurgled.

Cat looked at the wire in horror.

"Plug it in! Plug it in!" Tiger yelled.

Cat dived down, arms stretched forward.

"Do it!" Tiger cried.

Cat slammed the wire into the last vacant port.
The circuit board fizzed with energy.

Badlaw's voice boomed out again. "Two, one …"

Cat and Tiger flew out of the control panel and away from the energy wrench.

"FIRE!" yelled Badlaw.

Tiger hit the button on his watch just as the room was filled with a deafening *BOOOOOMMM!* Cat and Tiger closed their eyes and covered their ears.

When they opened their eyes, they found
themselves back on board the Excelsa, in the
teleport room. Before either of them could speak,
the whole ship rocked with the force of the
energy wrench as the beam hit the Excelsa.
They were thrown to the ground. All around
them, the walls trembled and shook.

"Are you OK?" Tiger asked Cat when the shaking stopped.

"I think so," Cat replied. "Were we just hit by a billion mega-whumps?"

"I hope so," said Tiger, as he got to his feet. "Shall we go and find out?"

Along the corridor, they saw Ant staring at
the communi-screen. As they made their way
towards him, they heard him speak into it.

"No sign of them yet," he said.

"OK. Keep a look-out," Max replied.

"Oh no!" Cat wailed. "He's still trapped
in the time loop!"

Ant turned away from the screen with a confused expression on his face.

"Cat? Tiger? There you are!" he said. "Where have you two been?

"Ant! You can hear us!" Tiger cried.

"Of course. Max just sent me to check on you. He was worried because Badlaw was nearby."

Tiger laughed. "We don't have to worry about Badlaw for a while. He's got problems of his own. He's just about to fly into a time rift."

"What?" Ant asked. "How do you know?"

"Just a funny feeling I have." Tiger shrugged.

Max spoke over the communi-screen. "Everyone to the bridge. We've somehow lost a lot of time. We need to get back on course quickly."

"Come on," Tiger said. "Let's go and join the others."

"There's no time like the present," Cat replied with a grin.

The micro-ship flew out into space, leaving Badlaw and the time rift behind.

Find out what happens next in
Double Cross.